Learning to Read, Step by Step!

Ready to Read Preschool–Kindergarten
• big type and easy words • rhyme and rhythm • picture clues
For children who know the alphabet and are eager to begin reading.

Reading with Help Preschool–Grade 1
• basic vocabulary • short sentences • simple stories
For children who recognize familiar words and sound out new words with help.

Reading on Your Own Grades 1–3
• engaging characters • easy-to-follow plots • popular topics
For children who are ready to read on their own.

Reading Paragraphs Grades 2–3
• challenging vocabulary • short paragraphs • exciting stories
For newly independent readers who read simple sentences with confidence.

Ready for Chapters Grades 2–4
• chapters • longer paragraphs • full-color art
For children who want to take the plunge into chapter books but still like colorful pictures.

STEP INTO READING® is designed to give every child a successful reading experience. The grade levels are only guides. Children can progress through the steps at their own speed, developing confidence in their reading, no matter what their grade.

Remember, a lifetime love of reading starts with a single step!

To Joshua, who was born finding words!
Love from Mom
—K.E.H.

To Twin B, my other half.
Love from Twin A
—D.K.H.

Text copyright © 2003 by Kathryn Heling and Deborah Hembrook.
Illustrations copyright © 2003 by Patrick Joseph.
All rights reserved under International and Pan-American Copyright Conventions.
Published in the United States by Random House Children's Books, a division of
Random House, Inc., New York, and simultaneously in Canada by Random House of
Canada Limited, Toronto.

www.stepintoreading.com

Educators and librarians, for a variety of teaching tools, visit us at
www.randomhouse.com/teachers

Library of Congress Cataloging-in-Publication Data
Heling, Kathryn.
Mouse's hide-and-seek words : a phonics reader / by Kathryn Heling & Deborah Hembrook ;
illustrated by Patrick Joseph. — 1st ed.   p.   cm. — (Step into reading. A step 1 book.)
SUMMARY: By dropping the first letter of a variety of words, Mouse makes several new
rhyming words.
ISBN 0-375-82185-6 (trade) — ISBN 0-375-92185-0 (lib. bdg.)
[1. Vocabulary—Fiction. 2. Mice—Fiction. 3. Stories in rhyme.] I. Hembrook, Deborah. II.
Joseph, Patrick, ill. III. Title. IV. Series: Step into reading. A step 1 book. PZ8.3.H41347
Mr 2003 [E]—dc21   2002009255

Printed in the United States of America   First Edition   10 9 8 7 6 5 4 3 2 1

STEP INTO READING, RANDOM HOUSE, and the Random House colophon are registered
trademarks of Random House, Inc.

STEP INTO READING®

STEP 1

MOUSE'S Hide-and-Seek Words

A Phonics Reader

by Kathryn Heling
& Deborah Hembrook
illustrated by Patrick Joseph

Random House 🏠 New York

Words are here,
words are there.
Little words hide
everywhere!

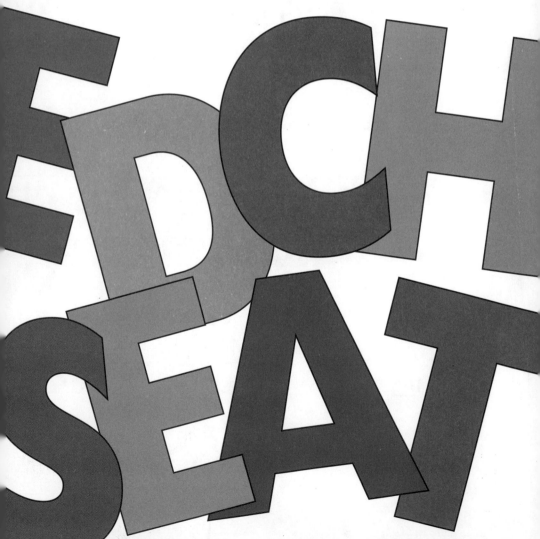

Look in big words.

Take a peek.

Find a small word—

hide-and-seek!

Mouse rides a train.

train

It starts to rain.

rain

Mouse gets a plate.

plate

He is too late.

late

Mouse pulls the string.

string

Now the bells ring.

ring

Mouse breaks his stool.

stool

He works with a tool.

tool

Mouse wants to stop.

stop

But he hikes to the top.

top

Mouse hears a shout.

shout

Crow yells,
"Look out!"

out

Mouse waters his plants . . .

plants

with help from ants.

ants

Mouse buys a treat.

treat

Now he can eat.

eat

Look at Mouse throw!

throw

He wins three in a row!

row

Mouse starts to trip.

trip

Oops! His pants rip!

rip

The sun is too bright.

bright

Now it is just right.

right

Mouse likes to spend.

spend

But this is the end.

end

Mouse's hide-and-seek
is done.

Playing word games
is such fun!

Keep on looking
here and there—
words are hiding
everywhere!